ABOUT THE BANK STREET READY-TO-READ SERIES

Seventy years of educational research and innovative teaching have given the Bank Street College of Education the reputation as America's most trusted name in early childhood education.

Because no two children are exactly alike in their development, we have designed the *Bank Street Ready-to-Read* series in three levels to accommodate the individual stages of reading readiness of children ages four through eight.

- ○ *Level 1:* GETTING READY TO READ—read-alouds for children who are taking their first steps toward reading.
- ○ *Level 2:* READING TOGETHER—for children who are just beginning to read by themselves but may need a little help.
- ○ *Level 3:* I CAN READ IT MYSELF—for children who can read independently.

Our three levels make it easy to select the books most appropriate for a child's development and enable him or her to grow with the series step by step. The *Bank Street Ready-to-Read* books also overlap and reinforce each other, further encouraging the reading process.

We feel that making reading fun and enjoyable is the single most important thing that you can do to help children become good readers. And we hope you'll be a part of Bank Street's long tradition of learning through sharing.

The Bank Street College of Education

To David Glenn Bunn III
— W.H.H.

To my mother and father,
with much love
— T.T.

For a free color catalog describing Gareth Stevens' list of high-quality books and multimedia programs, call 1-800-542-2595 (USA) or 1-800-461-9120 (Canada). Gareth Stevens Publishing's Fax: (414) 225-0377.

Library of Congress Cataloging-in-Publication Data

Hooks, William H.
    Lo-Jack and the pirates / by William H. Hooks; illustrated by Tricia Tusa.
        p. cm. -- (Bank Street ready-to-read)
        Summary: When Jack is kidnapped by a band of greedy pirates, he persists in misunderstanding all the captain's orders.
        ISBN 0-8368-1782-6 (lib. bdg.)
        [1. Pirates--Fiction. 2. Humorous stories.] I. Tusa, Tricia, ill. II. Title.
    III. Series.
    PZ7.H7664Lo   1999
    [E]--dc21   98-38492

This edition first published in 1999 by
Gareth Stevens Publishing
1555 North RiverCenter Drive, Suite 201
Milwaukee, Wisconsin 53212 USA

© 1991 by Byron Preiss Visual Publications, Inc. Text © 1991 by Bank Street College of Education. Illustrations © 1991 by Tricia Tusa and Byron Preiss Visual Publications, Inc.

Published by arrangement with Bantam Doubleday Dell Books For Young Readers, a division of Bantam Doubleday Dell Publishing Group, Inc., New York, New York. All rights reserved.

Bank Street Ready To Read ™ is a registered U.S. trademark of the Bank Street Group and Bantam Doubleday Dell Books For Young Readers, a division of Bantam Doubleday Dell Publishing Group, Inc.

Printed in Mexico

1 2 3 4 5 6 7 8 9 03 02 01 00 99

Bank Street Ready-to-Read™

Lo-Jack
and the Pirates

by William H. Hooks
Illustrated by Tricia Tusa

A Byron Preiss Book

Gareth Stevens Publishing
MILWAUKEE

4

Lo-Jack was his name,
but they mostly called him Jack.
He loved pirate stories.
But he knew nothing about real pirates.
"I'd like to sail the seven seas
and capture ships loaded with treasure.
The pirate life is the life for me!"
Then one dark night . . .

Jack was sailing his boat in the tub,
dreaming of life at sea.
Suddenly he was grabbed by two pirates!
"Don't move!" said a tall, skinny pirate.
"This is a hijack,"
growled a short, fat pirate.
"No, no," cried Jack.
"You've got the wrong lad.
I'm Lo-Jack, not High-Jack!"

But before Jack could yell "Help!"
he found himself on board
a real pirate ship.

8

"Just what the captain ordered,"
said the tall pirate.
"And just in time for the captain's
supper," said the other one.

Jack began to tremble.
"Oh please, sir," he said,
"I wouldn't make a good supper.
I'm too scrawny and tough."

"You're a strange fish,"
said the tall pirate.
"Now shake a leg. It's time to serve
the captain his supper."

11

Jack stood on his left foot
and hopped below,
shaking his right leg.
The pirates shook their heads.

"So you're the new cabin boy,"
bellowed Captain Grim.
"We'll have you whipped into shape
in no time.
Before you serve my supper,
bring me my cat-o'-nine-tails."
"Yes, sir," said Lo-Jack.
And away he went to look
for such a cat.

Jack returned, holding the ship's pet.
"Will this do?" he asked.
"It has just one tail.
But it is the only cat I could find."
"Ho, ho, ho!" roared the captain.
"I like a good joke."

15

"Now serve my dinner, lad.
I'm ready to shovel in my food."
"Let me help you, sir," said Jack.

16

As Jack cleared the table,
he heard Captain Grim shout,
"Hit the deck, men!"

Jack ran upstairs.
He found an oar and began
to hit the deck.
He wondered why the other pirates
were not following the captain's orders.

First Captain Grim frowned.
Then he pointed at Jack.
"Ho, ho, ho!" he laughed.
"Hit the deck!
This lad breaks me up!"
All the pirates laughed.

"Button your lips!" roared the captain.
"This is a pirate ship,
not a pleasure boat.
We're moving out.
Trim the sails!
Weigh the anchor!"

Jack quickly found a pair of scissors.
He began to cut the sails.
"Stop that!" yelled the tall pirate.
"Go help weigh the anchor!"

21

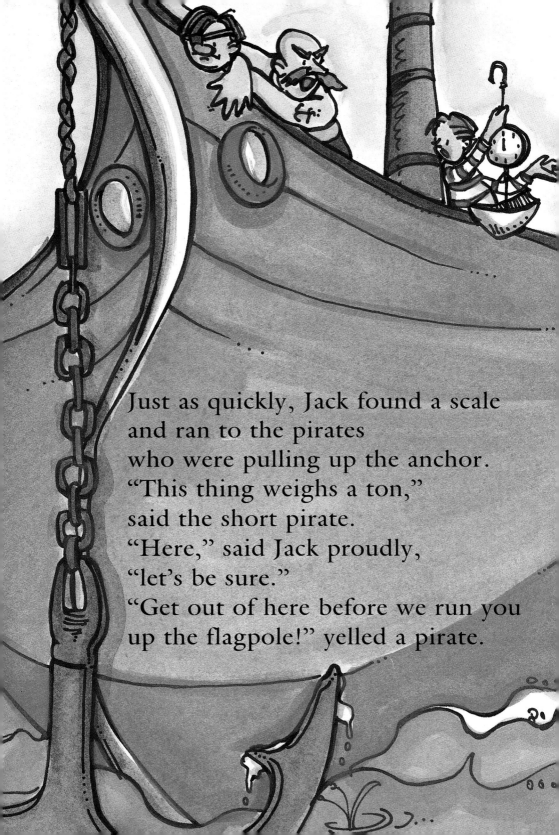

Just as quickly, Jack found a scale
and ran to the pirates
who were pulling up the anchor.
"This thing weighs a ton,"
said the short pirate.
"Here," said Jack proudly,
"let's be sure."
"Get out of here before we run you
up the flagpole!" yelled a pirate.

By the next day, the pirate ship
was far out at sea.

"Everyone must take a watch on deck,"
Captain Grim barked.
"Keep a lookout for treasure ships."

Jack searched high and low for a watch.
Finally he found one
on the captain's sea chest.

He ran back on deck with the watch.
"Skulls and crossbones!
What are you doing with my watch?"
asked Captain Grim.
"But, sir, you ordered everyone
to take a watch on deck," said Jack.
"I'm not laughing this time, lad,"
said Captain Grim.
"Put that watch back on my chest!"
"Yes, sir," said Jack.

Captain Grim was about to give
Jack a whack, when one pirate cried,
"Ship ahead on the starboard side!"
"Up to the crow's nest with you,"
ordered Captain Grim.

Jack looked all around.
He didn't see a nest of any kind.
"Up there, lad," said the captain,
shaking his head.
He pointed to a bucket high up
on the mast.

29

Jack climbed up the mast.
He shouted down to Captain Grim,
"Sir, there's no crow's nest up here.
But there is a gull's nest.
Will that do?"
The captain yanked at his beard
and turned red in the face.

"Give chase!" ordered the captain.
Jack soon spotted the ship.

"Can you see any arms aboard
that ship, lad?" called Captain Grim.
"Aye, sir," answered Jack.
"There are ladies' arms, gentlemen's arms,
sailors' arms, and even children's arms.
Everyone is waving to us."

"Then there'll be lots of treasure aboard that ship," said Captain Grim. "And they don't suspect a thing. Come down here, lad," the captain ordered.

"Pull up beside the treasure ship. Stand by to take her!"

Jack watched the women and children
waving from the deck.
Captain Grim yelled
through his bullhorn,
"SURRENDER THE SHIP,
OR WE'LL BLOW YOU TO BITS!"

The captain of the treasure ship
shouted back, "Never!
Never will I surrender my ship!"

"Prepare to fire the cannons!"
ordered Captain Grim.
Jack ran to one of the cannons
and built a fire under it!

37

"Surrender your gold, silver, and jewels, or we'll sink you," roared Captain Grim.
Poor Jack began to worry about all those nice people.

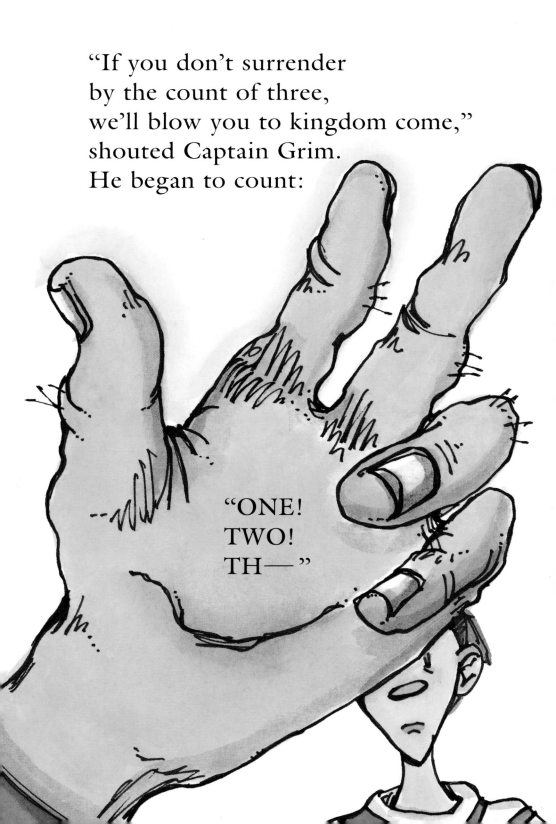

Suddenly Jack's cannon blew up!

There were pirates everywhere!

Captain Grim and the pirates swam
as fast as they could
toward a nearby island.
Jack found a plank of wood
and paddled toward the other ship.

43

A sailor yelled to Jack,
"Ahoy, lad. I'll throw you a stout line."
"I'm afraid of stout lions,"
answered Jack.
"But I would be ever so thankful
for a stout rope!"

"One stout rope coming down!"
called the sailor.

Soon Jack was hauled to safety.
The captain of the ship said,
"Lad, you blew up the pirate ship
and saved our lives.
You're a hero!"

That night the captain gave
a big party for Lo-Jack.
"A toast everyone! A toast!"
cried the captain.
"Let's raise a toast to our young hero,
who saved us from the pirates!"